MW00880290

Table of Contents

Chapter 1

Padded feet moved silently over freshly fallen snow. The large gray wolf stopped suddenly, coiling every muscle in its body. Less than thirty feet away a young elk nibbled on the few remaining leaves of a small tree. Unless something unexpected intervened, the elk would soon provide life-sustaining food for the pack.

The elk continued eating unaware of the wolves now ringing it on three sides. Crouching low, still moving closer silently, the large gray body bolted from its coiled position, leaping toward the blindside of the grazing animal. The other wolves, acting on the queue of their leader, followed immediately. The elk reacted within seconds to the movement of the large gray, darting rapidly to its right trying to avoid the attack. Unfortunately for the elk, this action placed it directly into the path of the other wolves. Within seconds, the animal was on the ground. Shortly after that, the attacking pack backed away for the leader to examine the fresh kill, to proclaim it fit for the pack to eat.

As the leader moved aside, satisfied at the prize, his mate stepped forward to quiet her hunger and the needs of her young pup, Flash. The other members of the pack waited patiently for this ritual of leadership to conclude so they might also enjoy the benefits of the hunt. Soon each wolf, bowing to their status in the pack, claimed their bounty.

The eyes of the great gray leader surveyed the antics of his pack from his position on a small rise. This wolf knew many dangers existed for him and his charges. When he was young, he experienced his first encounter with men. The encounter left him as the only survivor of his pack. His mother and father died as well as his older brothers and sisters. He survived only because he was so small the hunters missed him when celebrating the grand results of their shooting. The eight dead wolves provided an excellent trophy to tell about in the local pub.

His blazing yellow eyes flicked instantly as a strange scent brushed against his nostrils. There was no doubt, horses. Horses meant men. Men meant death. Without a sound, he loped to the pack and moved swiftly in the opposite direction from the smell. Each member moved as one, following their leader without hesitation. The smell of danger was so great the pack ran through the pine forest at their hunting speed. Hours later, the leader slowed to allow all to rest. On flat ground, a wolf could track prey at speeds reaching twenty miles an hour and maintain the pace for hours. The younger wolves would not find this gait possible, so the leader slowed to half that pace, keeping it the duration of their travel.

He found the highest point of ground and carefully let the air play through his nostrils seeking the telltale scents of all creatures. Many scents floated on the air except the one he sought, the horses. Their flight managed to put enough distance between them and the hunters. The air was clean and fresh.

Chapter 2

Flash's mother stretched out her full length, releasing a long sigh. Though he was over twelve months old, during the night he snuggled up tight against her for warmth. Her movement let his head drop striking the floor of the den, "Ouch." Flash did not want to wake up this way and tried to regain his nice warm spot. Mother looked at him, reached out playfully, licking him on the nose. That was one way to wake him. He used to like it when mother licked him but not now, he was too old. It was not the way to start his day.

"Mother, stop that, you know I don't like it."

She looked at him, letting her eyes tell him that he should be quiet. If she wanted to lick him, she would, she was his mother. Flash settled back on the den floor, this time against a wall hoping to get far enough away to find sleep.

He woke to find he was the only one in the den. Flash did not like that either. His morning was not getting off to a good start. First, he was forced to wake up, get licked, and then everyone abandoned him. He poked his nose outside, finding his family laying around grooming themselves. The recent snow had melted, the temperature was warming up, and Flash felt very comfortable due to the heavier winter growth of his fur.

He walked over to his oldest brother stretching out next to him, finding a slight spray of sunlight. Even this small amount of sun would gently warm his fur. It might be time for another nap.

Flash quickly reached the sleep he wanted, and soon the sun rose higher in the sky providing additional warmth to encourage his sleep. Flash's sister, his litter mate, also tried to relax in the Indian Summer's warm air. She did not have the same talent as Flash to relax fully and reach sleep quickly. She glanced at her surroundings multiple times, each time putting her head back down, trying to get a nap.

After a few minutes of this fruitless effort, Nieta stood suddenly. She looked around seeing her brothers and sisters still asleep. Her mother was busy with personal grooming, so she decided not to bother her. Nieta decided she did not like being awake by herself and walked toward the sleeping group intent on sharing her problem with someone.

All the wolves stirred slightly, all that is except Flash. He slept soundly not bothered by Nieta. This interested Nieta and bothered her. No one should be able to sleep that soundly. Without much delay, she walked to Flash, leaned close to ensure he still slept, then with a sudden movement nipped his ear with a bite hard enough to draw blood.

Flash yelped, jumped to his feet all the while rubbing a paw on the sensitive area. It hurt. Nieta stood close by, saying nothing. Flash took a few moments to access the situation, then realizing Nieta was the only wolf standing. He stepped toward her, and she backed away. Her action said, "I did it."

Flash jumped, and Nieta took off, running through the forest. Flashed delayed only a second then took off after her. It wasn't long before he was on her heels. He could easily catch Nieta but did not.

Flash possessed two attributes that set him apart from the pack. He could fall asleep more quickly or often than the others, and even though not fully mature he could run faster than any member of the pack except his father, the great gray leader. He followed Nieta for a while then became bored with following and decided to show her how fast he could run. A burst of speed propelled him by her. Flash chuckled to himself as he passed.

"I can run faster than anyone. I can. I can." Flash looked over his shoulder to gloat at Nieta. He turned around just in time to smack right into his father.

"What are you doing, Flash?"

Flash's answer was silenced by the force of his father's mouth grabbing him around the neck, firmly but gently. Carrying an almost fully grown wolf in this fashion did not seem to bother the great wolf. Flash's father dragged the embarrassed Flash passed Nieta heading toward where the pack rested. She walked with them, causing Flash to wish he was asleep in some secret place. It was terrible being dragged like a dead rabbit to be dropped in front of his family. Father walked through the pack right up to Flash's mother and released a somber young wolf.

"Where have you been, Flash?"

"Just playing with Nieta, Mother."

"I doubt if it was quite that simple son."

Flash's dad stood in front of him looking very tall and fierce. He reminded Flash that running wild in the forest could get him into big trouble if he ran into the wolf hunters. Flash had forgotten the warning but never felt he would find trouble anyway. He knew, however, if he was going to get away without a solid nip from his father he better agree with him and be quiet. He did both.

The scolding passed quickly, but Flash slipped quietly away from the others to find a secret place to be by himself. He was still embarrassed by what happened and a little angry at his father over being treated that way. Flash walked a distance from the pack so he could not see them, moving upwind so he would not catch their scent, then settled down feeling sorry for himself. He briefly thought about the run with Nieta, but only briefly before the darkness of sleep came.

Flash woke to strange sounds. He heard howls, yells, loud cracking sounds like tree limbs snapping under the weight of ice during the winter and then cries of pain. He stood, puzzled, looking for his pack. Flash stepped toward the noise when he heard new strange sounds. These strange sounds were mixed with other strange sounds, yelling sounds, excited sounds. He heard another wolf cry in pain followed by a loud crack. Suddenly, silence came. He did not know why but he knew something was terribly wrong. Something was wrong with his family.

Very carefully he walked toward the place where his family waited, a place that now had become quiet. Flash used the same stalking skill he would use to track a caribou. He did not know why but Flash knew if he were not careful something bad would happen to him.

Chapter 3

"Jim, look at this one, he's the biggest wolf I've ever seen."

The three hunters walked over their kills looking at each of the wolves they had shot. Pausing at each one, they pushed it with the gun's barrel to assure the animal was dead. Except for the large one, they all died with the first shots. Jim had to finish that one with another bullet through the head. It wouldn't matter, though, the bounty would be the same.

The scene was an old story for these men. Hunting wolves for bounty provided them with the income they could not get through any other means. The ranchers and farmers made it easy to live very well by bringing them the bodies of dead wolves. But lately, it was getting harder to find easy targets. There were fewer wolves this year than last year and less last year than the year before. Now a hunt took them away from home, The hunters had to travel further and further into the wilderness. It did not seem to matter to those paying the bounty if the wolf came from where they lived or not. For them, a dead wolf was the only good wolf.

Years earlier, all western states possessed wolf populations in large number and wolf hunters could get their quota easily. Now it was harder and took longer. "Have you guys noticed that this is the biggest pack we have taken this year and maybe last year."

Both of the other hunters grunted their agreement while continuing to skin the dead wolves for the pelts to prove the kill. To expedite the cleanup work, they leaned their rifles against nearby trees.

Flash arrived at the scene shortly after the men started the stripping of the wolves. He did not know what to do or exactly what had happened. He finally recognized his mother when one of the hunters lifted her head to start cutting the pelt. Flash whimpered.

The slight sound did not escape one set of ears. "Bill, look behind you. We have another wolf with us."

Bill turned slowly to peek toward where Flash thought he was hiding. He slowly reached for his rifle then whirled quickly firing toward the remaining wolf. Flash did not understand what happened, but he heard a loud sound, a whizzing noise and then pain on the side of his head. He fell to the ground when the bullet struck him, it left a half moon shaped hole in the edge of his left ear.

Another man now had his rifle, firing a shot toward Flash. This time the bullet missed. Flash scrambled to his feet and started running. He ran as he had never run before, faster, and faster he ran. Hours passed, and he ran. He left the pine forest traveling upward toward the mountain top, passed the peak into heavy snow, but he continued to run and run. Flash had no idea how long he ran but finally, his legs gave out, and breath came in short labored bursts.

With a mighty heave, Flash fell to the ground, sprawling out his full length, unable to move from fatigue. He lay there a long time until he regained his breath. Flash was not sure how long that was, but it seemed like most of a day. He got up to look for shelter. An outcropping of rock provided the barest type of den, but it was just what Flash needed. He placed his back against the rock wall, rolled up into a ball shape and went to sleep.

His sleep was restless, filled with the strange events of yesterday. The loud noises, the pained cries, seeing his mother's lifeless head in the man's hand followed by him being shot. Flash realized while running that his family was all dead. He has almost killed himself. The impression he carried from that day forward was that men were bad, evil and to be feared greatly. Never again would he let men get close to him. He would run and run, or if given no choice he would do as they did, he would kill. They would never again get the chance to kill him.

Flash woke during the late evening, startled by the howl of a wolf. He listened for a moment then turned his head to the sky answering with a long solid bay. Within moments other howls greeted his ears from many directions. Flash did not know what to think. He had never heard so many different voices at one time. In his family, they had once heard another pack, but that happened only one time. Where was he, why were there so many wolves?

Flash responded once more and heard an answer only a short distance away. He went in that direction. Within a few moments, Flash found himself in the midst of a large pack of wolves. He was a stranger, and they treated him as such. There were open suspicions from the pack. They looked him over, checked his scent, with each one letting Flash know they were the dominant wolf. Flash instinctively knew he had to assume a low position with each wolf and he did. He presented no challenge to any member of the pack, male or female. Satisfied the stranger was no threat, the pack ignored Flash, moving on, yet allowing him to follow.

As time passed life in the pack became good for Flash. Through interaction with the other members, his position changed. He grew older, now almost two, got bigger, about one hundred fifty pounds, but not driven by nature's urge to be the leader of a pack. Many wolves feel this urge but are unable to fulfill it due to lack of fierceness or strength. Flash did not realize the power nature provided him. He had become aware when the pack members started to challenge each other he was able to dominate all but the biggest male members.

In the third year of his life, Flash began to feel strange emotions. Spring came earlier than usual, and he felt restless, not sure what was happening to him. He found a desire to wander off from the pack, spending more time alone. The female members of the pack caused him to feel deep surges of something like anger but not quite the same. Flash did not understand what was occurring in his body or mind. He only knew when he met the pack leader, a giant white wolf, he no longer felt the need to express his subservient position. He did not challenge the white, rather he made sure they did not have to face each other.

Flash noticed one female, in particular, seemed taken with his attention. This wolf was two years old and made sure she was always near where Flash went. He began to feel the urge to mate, which before this time had not existed beyond normal curiosity. Now it was stronger. He approached the female and though willing she felt the need to make Flash work for her attention. This ruckus caught the eye of the white leader. While Flash and the female sparred, the leader stepped in front of Flash barring his fangs and growling low.

Flash stopped momentarily not sure of why the leader acted this way. The pause was brief then instincts took over, and Flash stood full height, posturing himself as a wolf intent on defending his territory. Flash was surprised by the deep low growl that came from his throat. The two fierce animals stood eye to eye with fangs showing, dripping saliva waiting for something to trigger what could be a death battle. The leader understood what was to happen, Flash did not. He only knew he had to accept the challenge as he had many others in the past. He never thought he would be challenging the leader of the pack.

Driven by some mystic timing, the leader lunged at Flash knocking him down while sinking his fangs deep into the challenger's throat. Flash suddenly understood this was different from previous challenges when one of the wolves would realize he was outmatched, give up and submit to the other. Flash summoned the untested strength nature provided, rising to his feet while carrying the leader still attached to his neck. Twisting fiercely, he shook the white loose, quickly closing on the back of the wolf's neck, feeling his teeth puncture the tough hide and tasting his first blood of mortal combat.

The fight lasted until fatigue challenged both wolves, with no particular winner. The white fur of the leader was marked with a lot of blood. Flash being grayer in color did not present such a marked image, but his wounds were as severe as the leader. During the battle, Flash realized he might be able to win, but was not sure. He was sure he never wanted it to start in the first place. His real interest was in the female not in fighting the white leader.

Exhaustion overtook both combatants, and they stopped to lie on the ground only a few feet from each other. Both were ready to continue the fight, but neither had the strength. Flash looked at the leader. He had been a great leader, and protector of the pack and Flash realized that it was time for Flash to leave the pack, seeking a life elsewhere. He got to his feet, the white did the same expecting the fight to resume. Instead, Flash turned, walked to the female, stopped to lick her face then continued walking toward the forest. The female followed.

Chapter 4

Flash and Marta roamed through the forest seeking their own territory. Working their way through the wilderness, they kept finding other wolf packs which drove them further and further from civilization.

It was evening and as Flash had done many times before he found a small rise, looked at the moon and howled. He listened to the sounds of the night for a response from another wolf. There was none. He howled again, and again the only answer was silence. He then knew this would become the territory for his pack.

The next day Flash and his mate wandered through the territory seeking scent marks to guide them as to where they would find the next pack. After covering about fifty miles, they started marking their territory for other wolves. This was their place, and they wanted it known to all others.

Flash and Marta searched their territory seeking a proper place for their den. This would be crucial for birthing the pups and raising them for the first few months. Flash would provide her with food during this period, and he wanted the den close to the best game areas. Hunting was easy since their territory was used by caribou and elk for passage on their trek from tundra to the pine forest.

The approach of winter brought an urgency throughout the forest as all creatures prepared to survive on a reduced food supply. Flash knew he would have to rely on his hunting skills to a greater extent to assure he and his mate survived the cold. Some internal instinct lets him know it was time for him to start his pack. That winter, Marta carried the first of many litters to seed Flash's pack.

In late February, the six pups were born. Marta was very attentive, and Flash remembered how his mother use to lick his face. For the first time in a long time, he thought about the day he got mad when she licked his face. He then remembered the day his family was killed by hunters.

Flash had not thought about that event or the men for a while. While these events played through his mind, he looked at his young pups, wondering about their future. He could provide a safe place for them today, but what about tomorrow? What would they face if hunters continued to kill wolves? Would they survive?

It was time for Flash to find food for Marta. Winter had chased most of the game to lower elevations, and Marta now needed more than rabbit or mice could supply. After leaving the den, he settled into his normal tracking gait, which would carry him past the borders of his territory where he could find a bigger game. Caribou or deer would be his choice.

Fresh scents crossing his nostrils indicated deer had recently passed. He stopped to check his location. He increased his trot to pursue the quarry. The scent became fresher, and he slowed the pace so as not to accidentally spook the game. The tracking took longer than he wanted yet shortly the scent was fresh, which meant the deer must be nearby.

Flash carefully searched for signs of the game. He saw nothing, so he carefully moved ahead. Suddenly Flash heard a sound that had brought terror to the heart of a young wolf. The cracking sound he heard when his family died.

This time he crouched into the snow, not moving, waiting. He pressed his head into the snow close to a dead tree and froze. He heard the strange sounds associated with men before he saw them. Then he saw two men walking through the trees, dragging a dead deer behind them. They passed close to Flash, but he did not move, though every muscle in his body coiled to spring in defense if necessary.

The men walked past, then Flash started following them at a reasonable distance. He found the camp, watching as they dressed the dead deer. Flash puzzled about these creatures. They did not look that dangerous, and he wondered why they wanted to kill wolves. When Flash lost sight of the men, his curiosity got the better of him, and he wandered into the camp for a look. As he passed a tent, one of the men stepped out. The man saw Flash about the same time Flash saw him. He froze when the huge gray wolf turned toward him, fangs bared and growls coming from his throat.

The other man who had been tossing a rope over a branch to string up the deer meat to protect it from predators entered the camp carrying his rifle. He immediately saw his friend's plight. In a steady, quiet voice, he said. "Harry, be still. I think I can get a shot at him."

Harry looked at Tom as he moved the rifle to shoulder height. "Tom, no, don't do that unless it turns on me. I don't think he wants me, I think he's as scared as I am."

The threesome stood there for a few minutes then Tom remembered the piece of venison he cut to cook for dinner. If the wolf were hungry, Tom would try to feed it. He slowly retrieved the venison from his pouch, tossing it in front of Flash.

Flash jumped when the meat hit the ground in front of him. The movement startled him, but he did nothing at first. But then he caught the scent of the meat and moved to sniff it closer. He was hungry, and it smelled good. With a quick movement, he snatched the meat in his teeth and bolted toward the forest.

Flash fully expected to hear the loud cracking sound he associated with men, but none came. He also remembered his ear and expected to feel pain with the noise. Neither event occurred.

He was not sure what to think of his encounter with the evil men. This time they did not try to kill him but gave him food. Not sure how to resolve this problem he left the men behind, carrying the food treasure back to his Marta.

"Tom, I told you wolves weren't dangerous."

Tom shook his head. "I don't know Harry. I never thought I would come face to face with a wolf in our camp, especially one that big. It must have been over six feet long and close to two hundred pounds."

"Tom, I think it got bigger as your eyes got bigger. It was a big wolf but not two hundred pounds."

Chapter 5

Flash reached the den happy he had something good for Marta to eat. She and the pups were fine and seemed glad to see him. The next morning Flash and Marta walked outside to view their territory. The snow base was starting to melt. Before long they would let the pups out of the den and move to the homesite Flash, and Marta prepared.

The months passed rapidly, and Flash now had a pack of seven wolves, Marta, and the six pups. He spent much of his time teaching the young ones how to survive in the forest, including practicing hunting skills. The litter of two males and four females grew rapidly, and by fall they were nearing full grown. Flash remained in his prime maturing into a great wolf leader. The previous encounters with men slipped from memory, and he did not spend time warning his pups about hunters as his father had. It was not necessary.

During this period the pack expanded as new lone wolves, and smaller packs met Flash and his pack. The initial period of greeting brought wariness from all parties as they assessed the other wolves or packs. This always first involved Flash as the leader of his pack. Lone wolves seeking a pack for protection and companionship did not create any concerns. When another pack traveled through Flash's territory, the initial encounter often went into aggression quickly. Both pack leaders had to determine the strength and leadership of the other. In the ways of a wolf, that meant they would need to fight.

Flash never encountered another pack leader that possessed his strength, size or speed. Any confrontation was short lived as Flash let the other wolf live. He had no desire or interest in harming another wolf or killing them to gain their pack. He let them go if they wanted as long as they left his territory. They never left joining Flash as part of his pack. Over time his pack grew in size much larger than he ever considered when he and Marta started their journey of life together.

Nature provided a place of safety for the Canadian wolves under the guidance and leadership of the largest wolf of all. Often Flash approached Marta to watch her mother the last of their litters. They both knew that time was going past and they must follow their destiny. Both knew that age would mean Flash would soon be challenged by a younger version of himself and lose his pack to another. It was the way of the wolf.

On this night the moon was bright providing light greater than anytime this winter season. Flash and Marta walked to the crest of a nearby hill to view the forest, mountains before them, their large pack scattered along the forest floor. He pushed his nose into her side gently letting her know he cared. Marta looked toward Flash, his face now reflecting white hair of age even in the moonlight. He turned to her, "We need to leave the pack soon Marta. We need to leave them with a new strong leader."

Marta knew that was true but not sure how that would happen. If they just left it would confuse the pack if he initiated a fight to give up leadership he could be hurt badly which would make leaving difficult. "How do we do that Flash? How?"

Flash looked toward a faint light glowing from the base of a nearby mountain. "I will indicate that I choose Fast to lead the pack before we leave. He is my son, the most capable to be the leader and the one I trust to care for the pack. He is strong, wise, and will help the pack grow." He moved a bit away from Marta, "Come with me Marta, we will leave tomorrow morning."

The next morning Flash took Fast with him toward the base of the mountain where he saw the glow the previous night. Flash knew that light came from men camping and he needed to let Fast know what that meant. Morning light arrived as the camp came to life with the hunters preparing their breakfast before starting the deer hunt.

Flash walked slowly, quietly as they approached the camp. Enough darkness remained for them to use shadows as protection as they watched the men. Fast not understanding what he was seeing but knew that Flash did so he just lay still. Flash turned to Fast, "Stay here Fast no matter what do not get up." With that, Flash walked slowly into the campfire light. He made no sound going unnoticed until almost at the fire. One of the hunters realized they had a visitor, a really large visitor. "Oh crap, Tom, look here quick."

Tom stuck his head out the tent to see what Harry wanted, "Crap, Harry I see it. What is it doing?" Flash did nothing except to slowly lay on the ground in front of the men.

"Harry that is as big as the wolf I gave the venison to a few years ago. Look at his face he is old enough to be the same one but could that really be?" Harry did not know, but he did know this animal give no indication of wanting to hurt them, fight. He just lay there looking at them.

Both men came and sat in front of Flash, but Tom had picked up his rifle which Flash noted but also saw he put it down. Though they had no idea what to do Harry said to Flash, "What you want boy?" He knew the question was wasted breath but not sure what else to do. Tom stood and reached for some jerky tossing it to Flash. Flash devoured it. Tom tossed him some more. Flash took it into his mouth, walked toward the woods and put it down. He then called Fast to come out.

When Tom and Harry saw Fast, nearly as big as the old wolf, they were concerned, but Flash stood between them and the other wolf so they could see what was happening. Flash gave the jerky to Fast who gulped it. Then they both came to the fire to lay down. Fast was not sure what was happening but knew he liked what he tasted. Tom took the remaining jerky and tossed it to both wolves.

Then without any notice, the wolves stood, so did Jack and Harry while Flash led Fast back into the woods. Just before losing sight of the camp Flash turned around, looked at both men and turning his head to the morning light greeting the day with a wolf song. These hunters had heard the song often but never like this. When he was done, Flash looked at the men again and disappeared into the forest.

Harry and Tom were totally numbed by what they saw. Though they never hunted wolves, never would for any reason, this encounter would stay with them for the rest of their lives.

Flash led Fast toward their territory stopping in front of Fast. "It is my and Marta's time to leave the pack, Fast. I want you to take over as the leader." Fast knew what he heard, that his Dad the pack leader was leaving and he would become the leader. The exchange was brief but no other communication required as this transfers occurred as it must. Later that morning Flash made sure the pack knew that Fast would be the pack leader chosen by Flash. Fast knew there might be others to challenged him, but he accepted that. It is what the pack leader must do.

Shortly after that Marta and Flash left the pack and their territory heading to the mountains a little further north where they would spend their remaining time. As they moved away, both considered their lives in a new territory. Flash and Marta placed their old territory in northern Canada where bounties on wolves did not exist. His pack could hunt and live there as nature intended without concern for the extinction facing wolves south of Canada.

Flash had no understanding of this difference, nor would he care. His only concern was for his pack. He cared that they had a chance to live, to be the hunter's nature designed for them. They did not kill for death or bounty as some men do, the wolf kills only to live.

Chapter 6

"Honey, could you give me a hand with this tent stake? It keeps putting out of the ground when I tug it." Jackie put the firewood down running to help her husband. Putting both hands on the errant stake, she looked at Ted. "Fire when ready Ted, I got this."

Ted smiled at this woman he found so beautiful and the mother of their four-year-old son. That summer they felt it was time to introduce Matt to the magnificent woodlands around their farm and the animals that made it home. "Here we go Jackie, hand on." Ted pulled the tent in an erect position pounding that stake into the ground before tapping the others to assure they would not have a midnight collapse.

Matt loved the camping trip. He loved the woods, he loved animals and right through his big eyes this moment in his world was absolutely beautiful. Ted glanced toward Matt to assure he did not wander into something that may make curiosity dangerous. The woods were safe as long as you understand what to do and what not to do. Six-year-old boys do not know that. They know to see, to touch then find out.

What their eyes see is exciting, what their eyes do no see is the potential danger. That is why Dads and Moms have their eyes on all things at all times to make sure the little hand that reaches out to touch something unusual come back safe.

The day went by very fast for Matt as he walked around the campsite with is family. Matt was the first child of Ted and Jackie though they wanted a larger family. After hiking down to the creek, tossing a few pebbles into the slowly moving water, they returned to their camp. Evening was starting to demand darkness with tree shadows stretching over the trail.

Ted reached over tossing his son's hair in a playful motion, "You ready for some of your mother's campfire special to eat Matt? It will be really good. After that, we can just sit around the campfire and tell stories about the woods and creatures that live there."

Matt turned around walking backward excited about the storytelling. "Dad, can you tell me a story about Wolves? I just love wolves and how they sing to the sky." Ted smiled, "Yes Matt, we can tell stories about wolves. I bet your Mom has a story or two about her wolf friends." Matt stopped walking to look into his Mom's face. "You have wolf friends Mom? Really?"

Jackie glanced at Ted with a not so friendly look. "Matt honey, I really don't but when I was a little girl we went camping one night, and while I slept we had a visitor come into our camp." Matt, just stood there not taking a step. "Would you tell me that story tonight Mom? Would you?"

Once again Ted got to see the Jackie look he would rather have left back at the farm. To help her he picked Matt up. "Well, if we don't get back to the camp we won't have any supper, and then we won't have time for stories about wolves or anything else. Maybe about bears or deer. There are lots of creature here with us now we just do not see them as they stay out of sight."

Matt thought about that a moment. "Why would they hide Dad, I like animals in our woods, I really do." Ted continued walking carrying his son. "I know you do Matt, but some people do mean things, and it makes the wood dwellers afraid of coming out of hiding." That made Matt sad as he thought about what Dad said. "Well, I will never scare or hurt a wood creature Dad, I just won't."

Mom got ready to cook their first campfire meal using her two burner propane stove. "Jackie, now that is what I call camping gear." Jackie still held the stove in her hand looking at Matt. "Matt you better tell your Dad to stop making fun of me or he won't get anything to eat, just you and me." Matt looked up at his Dad, "You hungry Dad? Did you hear Mom? Let's do something else."

Matt took his Dad's hand, and they walked outside the light of the fire. "Matt, this is the place we can often see any animals if they are near us. The darkness lets them think it is safe to be out here." Matt looked around eagerly anxious to see his first forest animal but saw nothing. "I don't see any Dad, not one." The disappointment in his voice came through clearly. His Dad just shook his head, "Maybe later Matt it might be a bit early yet."

They returned to the campfire as Mom said, "You guys want some hot chocolate?" Matt ran to his cup motioning to Dad to come on. "Can Dad have some?" Jackie almost burst out laughing as the serious tone in his voice. She reached down to kiss his forehead. "Of course he can Matt I was just kidding earlier." Matt looked at her not understanding then suddenly he did. "Oh, it's OK Dad come get some hot chocolate."

After dinner, his parents told Matt stories of their childhood, of animals they had seen. He listened with amazement of how they had seen all kinds of animals. Jackie reached out to take Matts chin in her hand. "Matt, ask your Dad to tell his bear story, the one about climbing a tree."

Ted looked at Jackie giving her the same look she reserved for him earlier. "Dad tell me the story, please." No dad can resist that type request, so the story began. Ted said when he was a few years older than Matt he went on a camping trip with his parents. During the night he left their tent going into the forest by himself. Some time later he heard a loud grunt right behind him and turned to find a bear standing taller than he was. The bear did nothing except sniff the air but when it came down on all four legs moved toward Ted, and he ran.

The bear chased Ted only because he ran it seemed later. Ted saw a tree ahead and started climbing. Looking down he was shocked to see the bear climbing behind him. Tel yelled as loud as he could, and the bear stopped. They just looked at each other neither moving. Suddenly Ted heard his Dad and yelled back. Dad came out of a thicket of trees carrying his only Henry rifle. He saw Ted up the tree the small black bear below him but not moving.

For a moment he felt this was a funny thing to see. His boy treed by a small black bear but then realized he needed to get his son down. He fired a shot just over the Bears head, and it dropped to the ground running off. Ted came down to a good scolding for leaving the camp area. He was scared, and so was his father. Upon the end of his story, Ted looked directly into Matt's eyes. "Do not ever leave the campfire area at night like I did. Do you understand?"

Matt understood what happened to his Dad and he would never do anything like that, never. "Yes sir, I do understand and will never do anything like that." He leaned forward, raised his shoulders shrugging away the thought of being chased up a tree by a bear. Matt was sure he would never do that, never in his whole life. Ted came over picking up the boy he loved so much that wanted no harm to ever come to him. As much as a parent wants to keep their children safe they can only do what they can. Matt would have to do his part as well.

Chapter 7

After story time it was time for sleep, and all went into the tent to sleep for the night. Dad, Mom next to each other and Matt on the other side of his mother. Sometime during the night, a noise woke Matt. He lay there and listened for a while. The loudest noise he heard was his Dad or maybe his Mom snoring, but he was not sure. He lay still listening as best he could to the sounds outside the tent.

Though now Matt knew it sounded like feet walking in the camp. He listened, not two feet like people but four feet like a dog. Matt remembered what his Dad said about not leaving the campfire area so he would not but wanted to see if some animal was in camp. Carefully moving so as not to wake his parents he moved the tent flap but saw nothing. That surprised him as he knew he heard something. He listened again, and the sound was gone. Matt decided to peek outside to see if any footprints were left.

Once again moving very quietly he carried his boots outside so he would not wake his parents. The campfire has mostly died which left little light for him to see but looking down he saw paw prints. He had no idea what kind but knew they had visitors while they slept. Looking down he followed the footprints in the ground unaware the faint campfire no longer provided the light to see the prints but the full moon.

Matt moved along focusing on the tracks he followed until he came upon the paws that made the tracks. Surprised more than anything else he looked up to see Flash and Marta standing in front of him. Matt knew these were wolves, they were large wolves. He turned thinking he would run then remembered his Dad's story about the bear, so he did not run.

Instead, he turned slowly intending to return to the camp but realizing he had no idea which direction to go. He turned back to the wolves who were looking at each other, then at him. He stood still scared to do anything as they came close enough for him to feel them breathe as they sniffed him all over.

Flash turned to Marta, "This is a human child like our litter. He is not dangerous, but he needs our help to go home. We can push him in the direction he needs to go toward the camp we saw earlier. If he is from another camp, they will get him there."

So the two wolves moved behind Matt pushing him in front of them as they walked him to the camp. At first, he did not know what they were doing then he did and starting walking to where they wanted him to go. In a few minutes, he saw the camp as the wolves just stopped at the edge of the light.

Matt was not sure what to do but thought calling his Dad was right, so he did. Ted woke to the sound of his son calling his name. Glancing over Jackie starting waking. "Where is Matt Jackie? Did he get up?" She had no idea but stuck her head out the tent quickly say, "Ted, get your rifle." He wasted no time picking up the Henry that belonged to his father joining his wife at the tent flap.

What they saw made both their hearts sink. Standing 20 feet away was their son with two giant wolves standing on either side and their son with his hand on the neck of the larger of the two. Ted finally found his voice, "Matt are you OK?" Matt just stood there nodding he was OK. "Can you just walk toward us son? We need to get you away from those wolves."

Matt started to move forward without either wolf moving. "Dad I got lost, and these wolves brought me back to the camp." Ted heard what his son said but did not believe it as it made no sense. Matt stopped walking, "I left the campfire following their paw prints not realizing how far I had gone and could not find my way back. I walked into the wolves without knowing it then they started pushing me with their noses back to camp. Once I knew what they wanted I just followed where they took me, and here I am."

Jackie heard the story but could not believe it. "Matt are you sure, they did not hurt you in any way?" Matt laughed a little before saying, "Well they smelled me over good and that was pretty scary but nothing else. There were very nice to me."

Ted put the gun down under the watchful eye of Flash who knew about guns from his pup days. Matt ran to his parents who hugged him tight. "Dad I remember what you told me about not running and I did not run. Then the wolves came up, sniffed me and brought me home." Ted hugged his closer so thankful he was OK and oddly rescued by two wolves. He turned to Jackie. "Hon, do we have any leftover hotdogs or hamburgers we can spare for these two?"

In short order, she found the remains of their meal giving it to Ted. He walked toward the wolves who had been laying on the ground, but both stood. Ted stopped tossing what he had in their direction. The food got a good sniff, and then it was gone. Shortly after that so were the wolves.

After stoking up the campfire a bit, all returned to the tent to finish the night. This time Matt got to sleep between his mother and father. Just before going to sleep Dad turned to Matt. "You now have the best wolf story of all time to share with others. I doubt if anyone has had the chance to be rescued by two great wolves. Matt knew that was true and the size of the two made him wonder just how big a wolf could be. He knew this from standing next to the one with the white face that it was a lot taller than Benji, their farm dog.

As they looped off on their continuing journey looking for a new home Flash and Marta both knew they made human friends that night. Both also knew they would not see them again, but they did not need to see them again. It was not in their lifestyle to be around humans as a pet. A wolf does not do that. What they did need to do was find a new place for their den.

Since they left the pack, their travels initially took them higher on the mountain. Once the tree line thinned, both knew they had to move back towards the woods for better hunting. They turned south still high in the mountains but closer to water, game, and places wolves like to hunt.

Without knowing the result of this decision until later it turns out their new home placed them closer to the family farm of Matt and his parents. Over time they found while out hunting one evening, they were close enough for them to watch as he grew older. Matt also would find out to his sorry that he would be close enough for him to observe the completion of nature's life plan for wolves.

Chapter 8

The camping trip turned out to be an excellent experience for Matt and the family. From that trip, he learned an enormous amount on how forest animals live and exist next to humans. The most unique part of this time was realizing that even the most fearsome creature does not exist just to hurt people.

As the years passed, Matt started school, reading as much as he could about what he saw first hand. It surprised him how many books were written about the bad stories of a wolf. When it came up in class, he would tell his story as other children made fun of him saying he just made that up to get attention. That bothered Matt a lot as he knew it was real. Even when he tried to get his teachers to understand they had little time for that discussion. To them most were sure that wolves were bad, a danger to humans and had to be destroyed if not contained.

Within six months of returning from the camping trip, he rode one evening with his Dad on the tractor to check out fencing on the other side of their farm. It was kind of far from the house, but Matt loved to ride the tractor and hoped one day his father would show him how to operate it. He knew he could, he just knew it.

On this particular Tuesday evening about 6 o'clock, they were riding down the line when Matt saw a movement in the trees. "Dad stop a minute. I think I saw something move in the woods over there." He point a little behind them and up a small slope. Jumping from the tractor, he ran to the fence as his father watched him. Suddenly Matt jumped up and down, "Dad, come here, you won't believe it, but I think I just saw a couple of wolves in the trees."

Ted jumped down running up to Matt. Looking along a finger point, he also saw the movement. They both stood still hoping whatever they saw would come out and slowly the saw a large head of a wolf appear. Shortly there was another head visible. Matt started smiling looking at his Dad. "I think those are the two wolves who led me back to camp Dad, I really think that is them."

Matt's dad moved closer to his son for assurance and to see more clearly what his son could see. In his mind, he remembered very clearly what they saw that night in the moonlight when their son stood with two wolves on each side. He was unafraid then though Ted did not share that comfort. Now, however, he also felt there was no danger and wondered if Matt was correct.

After all, this time had they just stayed in the area not moving on. Ted could tell at the time of the camp incident they were aged wolves which may have affected their behavior. Now he could see the white face of the larger wolf. The smaller female not yet there but she also probably was past litter raising. "Matt, we need to share this with your mother as she always felt the wolves you found that night protected you and I agree."

Then they turned toward the farm as they heard Mom ring the dinner bell. She still did that even though not necessary she just liked the sound. They glanced over their shoulder at the wolves who remained still until they got on the tractor then when Matt looked back they just vanished.

Riding back to the house Matt had a thought. "Dad, can we come tomorrow evening again and maybe bring them something to eat? I think they would like that and I sure would.? Ted thought that would be a fine idea to find out if they were still there which may mean they had been shadowed for a long time. "We sure can and see if Mom wants to come with us as I think she still feels they were taking care of you.

When Jackie heard about the wolves, she wanted to go see them, but Ted explained they had left but "We will go back tomorrow evening if you want to go with us and maybe take something for them to eat?"

The next evening the family got into their 4 wheel farm vehicle and headed out to the fence where the wolves were seen earlier. "Ted you think they are still here. It is very strange they came this way after what happened with Matt. I just cannot believe it."

Ted had given that subject a lot of thought and decided the two wolves were not seeking them out that for some reason just happened to come their way. If there was a purpose behind that plan, he doubted it had to do with the wolves. "Been thinking about that a lot myself but don't believe that they or us had anything to do with seeing them at the farm. What they did for Matt may have been a one-off event or due to something from their earlier life.

I just don't believe they came here seeking us. We just happen to be where they chose to make their territory. If you look at them, both have some years showing and expect left their pack due to that age seeking a place to live without causing problems for themselves or the other wolves. Based on the size of the white faced one expect he was the pack leader and either got defeated by a younger wolf or recognized it was time to let another lead the pack. He is big enough to be a leader but expect the years have the same result on a wolf as it does to us all. Makes us a little slower, a little less anxious to fight and the drive nature gives to be the leader tempers a bit."

Jackie listened as Ted spoke words that might be used to describe any number of people they knew. Both of them were still young, still vibrant and ready to take on any number of problems man made or something nature tossed into their lives. In 20 years of so it may be another story but not now. Right now raising Matt and his soon to arrive sister Kate would be their major goal for years.

Pulling up to the fence no one could see any signs of the wolves which was a great disappointment to all. "You think they will come?" Matt asked anyone who could hear him, but no one had an answer just peering into the woods hoping they might see them.

Ted got out followed by his family. Jackie brought the meat up to the fence handing it toward Ted. "You think we just ought to leave this here? I don't want to take it home again." Ted briefly considered options, "Come here Matt let me lift you over the fence. Take the food we brought and put it next to that big pine tree, right at the bottom."

Matt did as requested leaving the food on the ground hoping one of the wolves would come by to eat it. He could see nothing looking around on all sides. Walking back to the fence he climbed part way up, and his Dad lifted him over. They stood there for a while then decided the wolves must be somewhere else. Since they were already out Ted wanted to check out a corner post he noticed yesterday just as they saw the wolves. This time he want to get out and see if it needed replacing. Turned out to be solid, so they all headed back to the house.

As they approached the barn very distinctively, they heard the howl of a wolf followed by another howl close by. Smiling it made them happy to know they were still there. Maybe not part of the family as wolves never could be that but at least good neighbors. Climbing out of the 4 wheeler Ted closed the barn door taking Jackie's hand in his. "We have some new neighbors it seems honey." She smiled then as if on cue they heard may wolves answering each other echoing across the valley. Now they all laughed wondering what size family moved into their neighborhood.

Chapter 9

Flash and Marta continued searching for a territory they would call home as they knew they faced the last years they had. Flash still felt strong and with Marta's help finding game to eat never became a problem. What they felt might be problem would be defending their territory if another wandering pack decided to live here.

The thought was not of major concern as they explored the range they covered marking it for other wolves to know. Any wolf that came across their markings would know they were intruding and may be welcomed but knew it had no claim. Over the next few months, only a few wolf signs were found, and only one came to face Flash. This was a young wolf not near of size to challenge appearing to look for a pack.

Flash and Marta allowed him to run with them, hunt together and share their kills. They even allowed him to come close to the farm where the young human lived but let him know no one could harm those humans. At first, this made no sense until they found the first of many gifts left for them by these humans. Then Flash explained how they found the young human lost in the woods, led him back to his camp and how the parents gave them food.

"They wanted nothing else just thanking us for bringing their son back to them. Quite by accident, we found their farm is on the edge of our territory, and we make sure on our hunts we go by there. Often they leave us food wanting nothing in return. We like that."

Marta agreed, "We howl to let them know we have the food and to thank them for giving us this treat. It is a lot easier than chasing down a buck." She nuzzled up to Flash sharing her comfort. Flash enjoyed the companionship for a while then stood motioning to the others that it was time to travel the territory to assure no unwelcomed wolves were present. Part of that travel covered the farm.

Over the years that past since they help Matt find the camp he grew much larger, much like a young man. They knew this but also knew he remembered them and wanted nothing but to make sure they were OK.

Tonight they got to where they usually found the food earlier in their trek around the territory. Flash hoped there would be something but found nothing. They turned to head back into the woods thinking they would come by later when Marta, then Flash then the young wolf got a scent. Grizzley was nearby.

They moved silently following the smell coming their way from upwind. Slowly circling around they moved back into the woods using their best stealth walk. They had no desire to tangle with a Grizzly as it would be painful or deadly if that happened. Flash froze in midstep followed by the others. Ahead pushing against a tree trunk was a large male bear. They observed it for a while keeping downwind and silent. The bear gave no evidence of knowing they were there.

Flash moved to the left intending on providing a wide path around the bear to leave without it being aware they were there. All appeared to be going well until their young companion snapped a branch. The bear heard the sound stopping the tree rub turning in their direction. It did not take long for him to find the three. This was not a young bear and knew that wolves can be trouble, especially if in a pack.

He saw Flash knowing from his size he was the pack leader, then Marta and finally a smaller wolf, a young one. The bear did not want to fight the wolves. He might be able to hurt one or two, but three could actually hurt or disable him to an extent he could not run away, and that would be deadly. He moved toward them and received the warning growl from all three. They stood in his path daring him to come closer. The bear moved one step forward then stopped. There was no advantage to this fight. He turned and headed back toward the farm.

Flash looked at the others starting to head to their den when he realized the bear would find their food, maybe find the young human and that would be really bad. He turned back to the farm only to find the food, but his real reason was to do what they did before and keep the young human safe.

Matt arrived at the drop off point taking the food from the back of the 4 wheeler. He was almost 11 years old now and did many chores on the farm. He drove the tractor, 4 wheeler and other chores he got from his Dad. Tonight he asked if he could take the food to the wolves and without reason to think otherwise, they let him.

Matt placed the package on the ground by the fence post then used it to climb over. Picking up the package with the food he walked toward the tree where he normally left food. Tonight would not be different. He pulled the package through the fence picking it up and heading toward the tree.

The bear just happened to be passing nearby when he got an odor of the fresh meat. It had no idea about Matt, about what they did for the wolves he just smelled food. The bear saw Matt carrying the package and did not know what it was, where the smell came from and what he must do. He just wanted the meat, wanted it now and burst from the woods into the clearing growling loudly as Matt stood from placing the food on the ground.

Matt recognized the type bear backing away slowly as it approached him, then standing erect much taller than Matt it growled again. He was not sure what to do but running he knew was not the answer. He continued to back up as the bear passed the food allowing his nose to turn to the smell on the ground next to the tree. It dropped to all four feet heading to eat.

Matt thought this was his chance, so he backed up faster, turned his back to the bear to hop over the fence. The sudden movement startled the bear, and it turned in his direction, then charged toward him. There would be no escape for Matt he had no time to get over the fence and even if he did the bear would follow. He yelled for his Dad working on the garden not far away.

Tim heard the growls when the bear charged, he heard his son yell and then he heard the sound of attacking wolves. He ran toward the fight reaching to pull his son to safety. In front of both their terrified eyes, they saw a battle that happens in the woods between predators when things go awry. The bear stood tall with the wolves ringing it. Swinging with paws that could break bones the bear stood expecting an attack.

Without warning, Flash stopped the attack, backed up a few steps followed shortly by Marta and finally the young wolf who realized he alone faced the bear. The bear got the message it was a chance to avoid a loss for them all. It dropped to the ground started to walk away turning toward Flash to share it was better for them all. It definitely was better for them all to avoid a potential fatal fight.

Seeing the bear leave Matt tore out of his Dad's arms running to the fence. He knew these same wolves once again saved his life. He just looked at them, each one realizing the new wolf. Tim joined his son as this small pack came toward them sitting on the ground without a sound. Matt did not try to pat the wolves though Flash would not have minded that yet knew it should not be. The new wolf walked up to get a scent so he would know these humans in the future as it was important to his leader, it was important to him.

Then as if on cue they rose to their feet, walking to the food taking it as they left. Tim hugged his son realizing how close to being injured or killed he came if not for his wolf friends. They had a story to tell Mom and Kate though his sister was a little young to understand. As they entered the doorway, they heard the wolf howls echoing across the valley.

Jackie looked up from feeding Kate. "Anything unusual happen tonight?" The two men just looked at her, started to laugh, "Mom, you will not believe this, but I have a new and better story to tell. I know you won't believe this, but Dad saw it also."

As the wolves walked back to the den, Marta turned to Flash. "You always want to be a hero don't you dear?" He looked at her, "Did I make you proud?" It was time to eat and that they did, knowing what happened tonight was good.

Made in the USA
San Bernardino, CA
05 March 2018